MY ADVENTURES WITH

This book was especially written for
Dakota Durham

Adapted by Kate Andresen

ISBN 978-1-875676-52-1

The kingdom of Arendelle was a happy place.

But the king and queen lived with a secret worry. Their eldest daughter, Elsa, had magical powers. She could freeze things and create snow, even in summer!

Their youngest daughter, Anna, adored her elder sister. The two loved to play together in the snowy playgrounds that Elsa created.

Meanwhile in Nixa, Dakota Durham was waiting for her friends to arrive. It was June 18th, Dakota's birthday, and she was celebrating with a *Frozen*-themed party. Dakota was wearing a beautiful crimson cape. Larissa also came dressed as a character from the movie.

As they sat down to watch the *Frozen* movie, a warm glow from the TV screen lit up the room. Dakota became completely engrossed and soon found herself daydreaming that they were at the castle in Arendelle.

In her dream, she discovered that Elsa had accidentally hit Anna with a blast of icy magic!

The king and queen rushed the girls to the realm of the trolls for help. The trolls said that Anna would recover—she was lucky to have been hit in the head, not the heart.

Even though Anna got better, her parents worried that people would fear Elsa's powers. To keep her gift a secret, they locked the castle gates and never let anyone inside.

But whenever Elsa had strong feelings, the magic spilled out. Elsa didn't want to hurt her sister again, so she decided to stay away from Anna which made Anna feel very lonely.

When the girls were teenagers, their parents were lost in a storm at sea.

In Dakota's dream, she visited Arendelle whenever she could. It made Dakota sad to see that her friends, Elsa and Anna, had grown apart.

When it was time for Elsa to become queen of Arendelle, the castle gates were opened. Dakota and Larissa rode their horses through the gates and joined hundreds of people to attend the crowning ceremony. Elsa worked hard to control her feelings—and her powers!

Anna loved meeting all the new people. "I wish it could be like this all the time."

"Me, too," said Elsa.

At the coronation party, Anna met handsome Prince Hans from the Southern Isles. They danced and talked all night. He made her heart flutter. It was love at first sight so they got engaged.

Dakota was so happy when she heard that Anna and Prince Hans were to be married.

But when Anna told Elsa her plans, Elsa reacted angrily. "How can you marry someone you've just met?"

Anna argued back. "I can't live like this anymore!"

Elsa got upset and an icy blast shot from her hand—in front of everyone!

Worried that her secret was exposed, and afraid she would hurt someone, Elsa fled from the castle.

Dakota and Larissa stared in disbelief as they watched Elsa flee.

Everything Elsa touched turned to ice. "Stay away from me!" she warned the townspeople.

The kingdom was in an uproar as ice spread everywhere.

Suddenly, Anna understood why Elsa had been acting distant for all those years. She had to hide her magic!

Anna decided to go after Elsa. But as Anna galloped through the fierce wind, her horse threw her into the snow and ran off back to Arendelle.

As Dakota and Larissa were riding through the castle gates, Anna's horse galloped past them. But where was Anna?

"Quick!" shouted Dakota to Larissa. "We must find Anna!"

They re-traced the horse's tracks which eventually led them to a shop.

Inside they found Anna and a young ice harvester named Kristoff, and his reindeer friend, Sven. Kristoff agreed to help them look for Elsa.

Together, they set off up the North Mountain.

As they neared the top of the mountain, they discovered a beautiful wintery landscape.

There, they met an enchanted snowman named Olaf. Anna thought he looked familiar and asked, "Olaf, did Elsa build you?"

Olaf smiled. "Yeah. Why?"

"Do you know where she is?" asked Dakota.

"Yeah. Why?" replied Olaf.

Kristoff explained. "We need Elsa to bring back summer."

Olaf was eager to help them. "Come on!"

Meanwhile, back in Arendelle, Hans was hard at work helping the townspeople. When he discovered Anna's horse had returned without her, Hans turned to the crowd and said, "Princess Anna is in trouble. I need volunteers to go with me to find her!"

Soon, Hans and some soldiers set out in search of Anna—and Elsa.

Back on the mountain, Olaf led Anna, Kristoff, Dakota and Larissa to a giant ice palace that Elsa had created with her magic powers.

Elsa wasn't happy to see Anna. She was afraid of hurting Anna with her icy powers.

But Anna explained that Arendelle needed Elsa's help. The kingdom was freezing and no one knew what to do.

Now Elsa was frightened. She admitted that she couldn't unfreeze the kingdom because she didn't know how!

The two girls argued. Although Elsa didn't intend to hurt Anna, she hit her sister in the chest with a blast of ice.

Dakota and Kristoff rushed to help Anna.

Anna stood up and looked at Elsa. "I'm not leaving without you, Elsa."

"Yes, you are," replied Elsa.

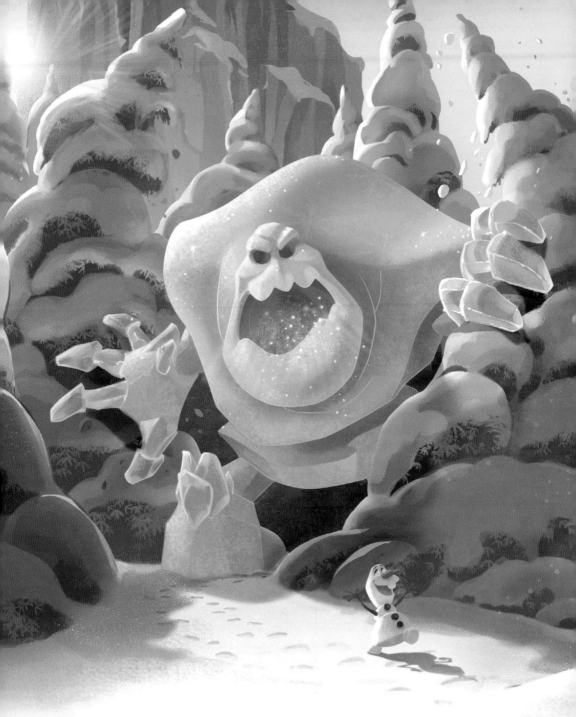

Elsa used her magic to create a huge snowman. He chased the friends out of the palace toward a cliff.

Luckily Kristoff had a rope. Dakota and Larissa quickly lowered themselves down the cliff.

When Anna, Kristoff and Olaf started the descent, the snowman grabbed the rope and pulled them back up.

Anna cut the rope and they landed safely on the fluffy snow below.

But something was wrong with Anna. Her hair was turning snowy white!

"It's because she struck you with her powers, isn't it?" Kristoff asked.

As night fell, he led Anna, Dakota and Larissa into a remote valley. He hoped his friends, the trolls, could help Anna.

One troll told them that Elsa's icy magic had struck Anna's heart. If the magic was not reversed, Anna would freeze completely! But, he added, "An act of true love will thaw a frozen heart."

The friends decided to take Anna back home. Surely Prince Hans could break the spell with a true love's kiss.

As they hurried toward Arendelle, Anna began to shiver. Kristoff was especially worried about her.

At that same moment, Hans and the search party arrived at the ice palace and attacked Elsa. As she defended herself, Elsa trapped one of her attackers behind icy spikes.

Hans cried out to her. "Queen Elsa! Don't be the monster they fear you are."

Elsa paused, but in her moment of doubt, she was knocked out. The attackers brought her back to Arendelle and threw her in the dungeon.

When they arrived in Arendelle, Anna thanked her friends for bringing her home safely.

Dakota was reluctant to leave, but she was sure that Anna would get better when Hans kissed her.

As Kristoff watched Anna disappear into the castle, he realized that he cared deeply for her.

Anna found Hans and explained what Elsa's icy blast had done and how his kiss could cure her. But he refused! He had only pretended to love Anna in order to take over Arendelle.

Hans left Anna alone and shivering.

Luckily, Olaf found her and lit a fire to keep her warm. But Anna was still getting weaker and weaker.

As Anna told him about Hans' evil plan, Olaf glanced out the window and saw Kristoff racing toward the castle. He knew that Kristoff loved Anna, so his kiss could still save her. With the last of her strength, Anna struggled outside.

Dakota and Larissa were almost at the castle gates when they saw Anna running toward Kristoff.

Then, Dakota saw Elsa run out of the castle and collapse in the snow. Hans stood behind her and was about to strike Elsa with his sword.

Seeing that her sister was in danger, Anna raced toward Elsa and threw herself in front of her. Hans' sword came down just as Anna's body froze to solid ice.

With a loud CLANK, the blade shattered.

Stunned, Elsa threw her arms around Anna and cried. She didn't want to lose her sister.

Suddenly, Anna began to thaw! Anna's act of true love for her sister meant that the spell was broken.

At that very moment, Dakota woke with a start. She rubbed her eyes and looked around her. Larissa was sitting next to her, and on the TV, she saw Elsa and Anna in a warm embrace.

Olaf watched the sisters and remembered what the wise old troll had said: "An act of true love will thaw a frozen heart." Anna's love for Elsa had saved both of them—and the kingdom.

Soon, the sisters were best friends again. With summer restored, Arendelle returned to normal—but now the castle gates were open for good! Kristoff decided to stay, and so did Olaf—with the help of a little snow cloud to keep him cool.

The sisters smiled at each other. Now everything was the way it was supposed to be.

This personalized Disney Frozen book was especially created for Dakota Durham of Nixa.

If Dakota loved starring in this personalized My Adventure Book then there are many more exciting stories in our collection.

Simply visit us at www.DisneyStore.com to create Dakota's next adventure!